MW00906645

Your Daddy Was Just Like You

By **Kelly Bennett** Illustrated by **David Walker**

G. P. Putnam's Sons • An Imprint of Penguin Group (USA) Inc.

With love and thanks to my critique buds: Ginny, Kathy, Linda, Marilyn, Marty, Pam, Peggy, Russell, and Varsha—"Flootles" all. And one extra-big hug to Ellen Yeomans for noticing what was underneath.
K.B.

G. P. PUTNAM'S SONS
A division of Penguin Young Readers Group. Published by The Penguin Group. Penguin Group (USA) Inc., 375 Hudson Street, New York, NY 10014, U.S.A. Penguin Group (Canada), 90 Eglinton Avenue East, Suite 700, Toronto, Ontario M4P 2Y3, Canada (a division of Pearson Penguin Canada Inc.). Penguin Books Ltd, 80 Strand, London WC2R 0RL, England. Penguin Ireland, 25 St. Stephen's Green, Dublin 2, Ireland (a division of Penguin Books Ltd.). Penguin Group (Australia), 250 Camberwell Road, Camberwell, Victoria 3124, Australia (a division of Pearson Australia Group Pty Ltd). Penguin Books India Pvt Ltd, 11 Community Centre, Panchsheel Park, New Delhi - 110 017, India. Penguin Group (NZ), 67 Apollo Drive, Rosedale, North Shore 0632, New Zealand (a division of Pearson New Zealand Ltd). Penguin Books (South Africa) (Pty) Ltd, 24 Sturdee Avenue, Rosebank, Johannesburg 2196, South Africa. Penguin Books Ltd, Registered Offices: 80 Strand, London WC2R 0RL, England.

Text copyright © 2010 by Kelly Bennett. Illustrations copyright © 2010 by David Walker. All rights reserved. This book, or parts thereof, may not be reproduced in any form without permission in writing from the publisher, G. P. Putnam's Sons, a division of Penguin Young Readers Group, 345 Hudson Street, New York, NY 10014. G. P. Putnam's Sons, Reg. U.S. Pat. & Tm. Off. The scanning, uploading and distribution of this book via the Internet or via any other means without the permission of the publisher is illegal and punishable by law. Please purchase only authorized electronic editions, and do not participate in or encourage electronic piracy of copyrighted materials. Your support of the author's rights is appreciated. The publisher does not have any control over and does not assume any responsibility for author or third-party websites or their content. Published simultaneously in Canada. Printed in the U.S.A.

Design by Richard Amari.
Text set in Sinclair Medium Script.
The art was created using layers of acrylic paints on paper.
Library of Congress Cataloging-in-Publication Data
Bennett, Kelly. Your daddy was just like you / Kelly Bennett ; illustrated by David Walker. p. cm. Summary: A grandmother describes to her grandson how his father was just like him when he was a child, never wanting to take a bath, fearing the dark, and swooping through the house in a cape and mask. [1. Fathers and sons—Fiction. 2. Behavior—Fiction. 3. Grandmothers—Fiction.] I. Walker, David, 1965– ill. II. Title. PZ7.B4425Yo 2010 [E]—dc22 2008053644

ISBN 978-0-399-25258-7
3 5 7 9 10 8 6 4

For Max, forever my baby.

K.B.

For my dad.

D.W.

Your daddy

was born puny and red-faced.

Just like you.

First he crawled,

then he tippy-toddled.

He said, "Oogie, boogie, bah bah lou."
Just like you.

Your daddy had two favorite friends,
Raggedy and Bear.
Together they went everywhere.

"Time for your shot," said the doctor.
"Bear first, Bear first," said your daddy.
Just like you.

When he started school,
your daddy said:

"IT'S HARD"
and
"DO I HAVE TO?"

Just like you.

He counted on his fingers.

He missed questions
on tests.

He forgot his homework.

But your daddy practiced.
And learned.
And kept getting smarter
and smarter and smarter.
Just like you.

Your daddy was zippy and sharp-eyed.

Just like you.

He loved games, but he didn't always win.

Sometimes he got mad when he lost.

Sometimes he cried.

Later, he always wanted to play again.

Most days your daddy was
my sweet boy.

But some days he turned
into a wild thing.

He raised a ruckus.

He crashed. He teased
or bossed or bashed.

He fumed

and fussed.

On those days,
your daddy was sent to
TIME-OUT.
Just like you.

Some days
your daddy was a race car,

or a gorilla.

Then he was a cowboy,

or he swooped through the house
in a cape and mask.

Sometimes I mistook him for
Stinky Swamp Man.

Your daddy never wanted to take a bath.
But once he was in the tub,
he never wanted out.

He splashed and sang.
And made himself sudsy disguises.
Just like you.

Your daddy wasn't always brave,
especially at night.

Spookies clanked
in the closet.

Creepies crawled
under the bed.

He checked and rechecked,
flashed the lights
and bounced three times.

I said, "Nighty-night, sleep tight."

He said, "Keep the door open, just a crack."

Just like you.

Every morning, when your daddy woke up,
I gave him a big hug and smooch.
And said a prayer of thanks that he was mine.

Your daddy is my baby.
And no matter how big he gets, or how old he gets,
he will always be my baby.

Just like you.